3.0

Delton, Judy
I'll Never Love Anything Ever Again